Mae Jemison
and Her Dream

by Meish Goldish
illustrated by Kristin Barr

Harcourt

Orlando   Boston   Dallas   Chicago   San Diego

Visit *The Learning Site!*

www.harcourtschool.com

　　As a young girl, Mae Jemison loved to read books about science and space. She dreamed about how much fun it might be to fly into space.

　　Mae didn't know yet that one day she would really achieve that feat!

When Mae was 12, a wonderful thing happened. In 1969, two U.S. astronauts landed on the moon. They were the first people ever to reach the moon and walk on it.

Mae was very excited about the moon walk. She read and reread all about it.

Space and science were Mae's great interests. However, she liked many other things, too. In high school, she studied dance and art. She acted in school plays. She even led cheers on the school cheerleading team.

Mae decided to study medicine and become a doctor. She also studied other subjects. She took classes to learn more about her own people, African Americans. She learned to speak Russian, Japanese, and Swahili.

When Mae went to work in West Africa in 1982, she was already a doctor. She wanted to help the poor people there.

The people of West Africa were very happy to have Mae. They showed her great hospitality.

Mae worked in West Africa for more than two years. She then returned to the United States to work as a doctor here.

All the time, Mae never lost her interest in space. She dreamed of flying some day.

In 1983, Sally Ride became the first American woman to fly in a space shuttle. Sally was a real heroine to Mae. Her feat made Mae want to go into space even more.

Mae applied to NASA, the National Aeronautics and Space Administration, and hoped she would be chosen for a shuttle mission.

SPACE SHUTTLE EXPLODES!

Then, in 1986, a very sad thing happened. A NASA space shuttle exploded in the air. Seven astronauts were killed. One of them was a woman, Christa McAuliffe.

Christa, like Sally Ride, had been a heroine to Mae. Mae was very upset, but she refused to give up her dreams of space.

In 1987, Mae was invited to train at NASA. She was glad to be asked, but she knew the hard part was yet to come. She would have to be trained and tested for a year. Did she have what it takes to fly on a space shuttle?

In one test, Mae rode in a jet. The plane soared high and then fell fast. In this "free fall," Mae floated inside the plane for a short time. It showed her how she would feel flying in space.

Many astronauts grew very sick when they went into free fall. Mae felt fine.

Mae was pretested, tested, and retested to see if she could survive hard times. In one test, she had to live in the wild for three days with little food. If her shuttle landed in the wrong place, she might really have to live that way!

In another test, Mae had to stay in a zipped-up ball for two days until help came. This test was to make sure she wasn't afraid of the dark or small spaces.

By the end of a full year, Mae had stood up to every test. She was now ready to fly!

For the next four years, Mae trained for her space trip. She practiced the jobs she would perform while on the space shuttle.

In 1992, the big day came at last. Mae was part of a crew of seven. Thousands of spectators stood and cheered as the space shuttle *Endeavor* soared into space.

On the shuttle, Mae performed many tests. She watched how frogs grew from eggs while floating. She studied how bone cells of men and women grew in space.

Mae also studied what made people feel sick in space. Being a doctor made her perfect for her job as a mission specialist.

The shuttle flew in space for eight days. When Mae returned, she was a heroine around the world. She was the first African American woman ever to fly in space.

Mae showed that, with hard work, the dreams of a young girl can come true.